fish heads and fire ants

This is a down-to-earth, funny book about two boys who learned that getting along with one another was not so great a problem as coping with the adversities of nature.

Paired together on a three-day survival camping trip, Harvey and Rocky are about as different from each other as possible. Harvey is slight, tidy, a worrier. Though younger, Rocky is bigger, messy, and carefree. They get off to a predictably bad start when Harvey tries to get Rocky to pick up his dirty clothes. "I'm camping with my mother!" Rocky explodes. "I'm camping with my mother!"

But gradually, the task of camping in the woods on their own begins to absorb them. Before they are fully aware of what has happened, each is helping the other when conditions demand co-operation, and in the process, each boy discovers qualities about the other that he can accept and admire.

FISH HEADS
and
FIRE ANTS

by george s. cook

illustrated by h. b. vestal

YOUNG SCOTT BOOKS

Library of Congress Cataloging in Publication Data

Cook, George S   1920–
   Fish heads and fire ants.

SUMMARY: In spite of their differences two boys on
a camping trip learn to cooperate so they can pass a
three-day survival test in the woods.
[1. Camping—Stories]   I. Vestal, Herman B.,
          illus.   II. Title.
PZ7.C7696Fi   [Fic]   72-10111
          ISBN: 0-201-09230-1

Contents

1.
The Echo

Harvey stood on a large rock at the north end of the island. Waving farewell, he watched Mr. Adams row his boat around the bend of the river.

He felt a small tremor of fear and loneliness. This was the first time in his life that he would be really all on his own.

Learning how to camp and survive in the woods during the training program of the last month had been fun. He knew he had learned a lot. But still, he wondered if he could pass this three-day test of doing it all on his own.

Taking a deep breath to calm his fears, he climbed down from the rock and pushed through the brush to reach their camping gear by the shore. He glanced at Rocky, who was still playing catch with his wet towel.

He just knew that Rocky was going to be difficult. He couldn't understand why he had been stuck with him as a camping partner. In his heart he really knew why, but he just didn't want to admit it.

Rocky threw his wet towel in the air and ran to catch it. The water squished out of his shoes. The wet pants clung to his brawny legs as more water dripped from his shirt pocket.

"Hooray! Three whole days! Three days with nobody telling me what to do. Three days of fun!"

Rocky was bigger and stronger than Harvey, even though he was not yet eleven. And it was just like Rocky to fall in the river while they were docking the boat. Rocky's black hair dripped with water as he wiped his big tanned face with the dirty towel.

"Rocky," Harvey called, with a trace of annoyance in his voice. "Put on some dry clothes."

Rocky whirled. The towel plopped to the ground. He stomped over to Harvey, the bubbles of water oozing from the seams of his shoes.

8

"Let's get one thing straight, Harvey. You may be older, but I'm bigger. You ain't telling me what to do. Understand?"

Harvey glared back at Rocky, who stood half a head taller. He knew he couldn't match Rocky's strength or weight. He couldn't speak and yet he couldn't back down.

Rocky stepped closer. The end of his nose almost touched Harvey's nose. He clenched his fists. "I can lick you!"

Harvey blinked. Still facing Rocky, he stepped to one side. "What would that prove? We're stuck with each other for three days. Why don't we make the best of it?"

Rocky continued to glare, but he unclenched his hands. "Okay. But just don't tell me what to do!"

Harvey's eyes dropped for a moment as he, too, relaxed. "Sure, Rocky. I'm not trying to tell you what to do." He pointed to the wet clothes. "I just don't want you to catch cold. If you get sick, we'd have to call the base camp. Then Mr. Adams would come and take us off the island. You don't want them to take us off the island, do you, Rocky? I want the three days, too."

"I won't get sick. I'm not a puny sack of bones like you are, Runt."

Harvey ignored the insult. "But you might. Put on some dry clothes. I don't want you to get sick."

"Bah! Why don't you just shut up. If it will

make you feel any better, I'll just take these wet clothes off."

Quickly, Rocky unbuttoned his wet shirt, peeled it off and threw it over a bush. Sitting down on the ground, he clawed at the wet laces of his shoes, but he couldn't undo the knots. At last, he forced the shoes from his feet and exposed his toes through the gaping holes in his dirty gray socks. He stripped off the socks and tossed them to a bush where they hung for a moment before falling to the ground.

Harvey became nervous. His eyes searched the river banks. "Are you going to change right out here in public? Let's get the tent up first."

Rocky rose to his feet and undid his belt. "Tent? Public? Who's there to see? I don't see nobody. Nobody but you. You won't tell, will you, Harvey? After all, you don't want me to get sick."

He unzipped his pants and pulled them off. Water, still in the roll of the cuff, trickled to the ground. Holding his pants by one leg, he whirled them around his head before flipping

11

them to the low branches of a nearby tree. Then, stripping off his wet underpants, he held them high in the air.

"You happy now? See? I'm not wet. I won't catch cold."

High up on the cliff on the Wisconsin shore, a flash of light caught Harvey's eye. "Rocky! Put on some clothes. There are people up there."

Rocky quickly crouched down behind a bush. "Where? Where? I don't see anything."

"It's a bunch of girls. Looks like maybe a bunch of girl scouts or something."

"Who cares," Rocky snorted. He clung to the bush, his eyes searching the cliff. "Toss me my knapsack, will you?"

Harvey picked up the bag and tossed it to Rocky. He opened it, dumped the contents on the ground, and fished around for his bathing trunks. He put them on.

"Now, Harvey, are you happy?"

He stepped into the clearing for a better look at the cliff. There were some kids playing up there, but they were a long way off. He shrugged his shoulders and turned back.

12

"You think now I won't catch cold?"

Harvey nodded, but wrinkled his nose in disgust as he looked at Rocky's dirty feet and the pile of dirty clothes.

"Yes, I'm happy. But I was wondering. When was the last time you had a bath? And look at this island. You've got your dirty wet clothes thrown all over it. And look at the stuff from your knapsack. Don't you ever wash your clothes? Can you really put on such filthy clothes?"

Rocky's face got redder and redder. He slapped his forehead with the palm of his hand and stomped in a circle. "I'm camping with my *mother!* I'm camping with my mother. For three days, I'm stuck camping with my mother. What did I ever do to deserve this? Here I have three days. Three whole days. All to myself. Do what I want, when I want, and how I want. And what do I find? I'm camping with my mother!"

Harvey glared back. "Don't be an idiot. I'm not your mother. It's just that—"

"Just that—what?"

"Just that we've got to set up camp."

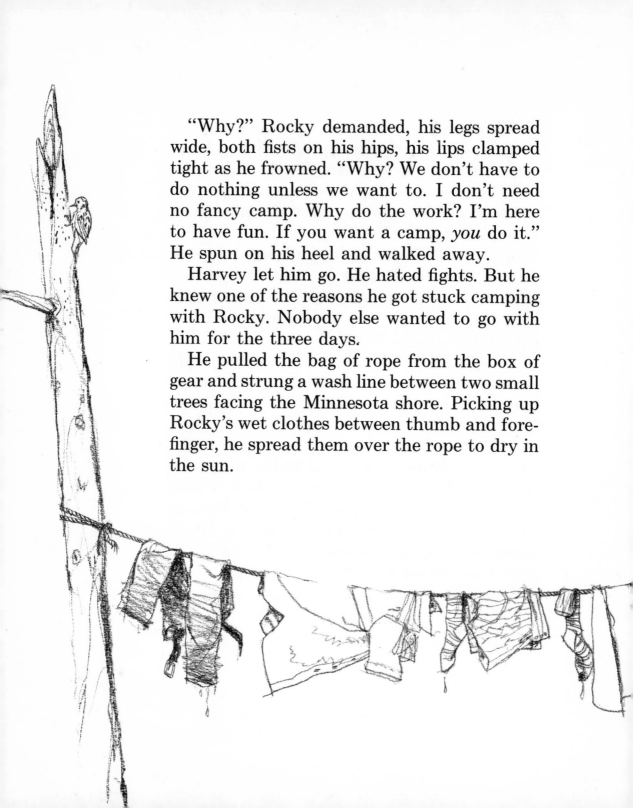

"Why?" Rocky demanded, his legs spread wide, both fists on his hips, his lips clamped tight as he frowned. "Why? We don't have to do nothing unless we want to. I don't need no fancy camp. Why do the work? I'm here to have fun. If you want a camp, *you* do it." He spun on his heel and walked away.

Harvey let him go. He hated fights. But he knew one of the reasons he got stuck camping with Rocky. Nobody else wanted to go with him for the three days.

He pulled the bag of rope from the box of gear and strung a wash line between two small trees facing the Minnesota shore. Picking up Rocky's wet clothes between thumb and forefinger, he spread them over the rope to dry in the sun.

He slung his knapsack over his shoulder and strode up the path that sloped gently upward to the top of the island. On the crest of the hill, he found a clearing under the pines and oaks. He dropped his knapsack at the base of a tree.

From the crest of the twenty-foot hill, Harvey looked over his island—his home for the next three days. Except for this clearing, pine, oak, and spruce trees almost covered the island. All of the island could be reached by several paths that cut through the under-growth of tree seedlings, hazel, and pricker bushes. The sandy soil made a soft, fertile ground for the violets and wild geraniums that spread their fragrance into the quiet, warm air. Harvey figured that the island was about 200 feet long by about 100 feet wide.

The south end of the island was built up with many boulders. He could see Rocky crawling over and around them exploring the holes and caves that they made.

Returning to the beach, Harvey tugged and pulled the five-gallon can of water to the camp.

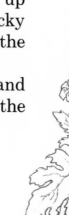

Again from the crest of the hill, he watched the island split the river. Most of the current went to the Wisconsin shore which was over 150 feet away.

The Wisconsin shore rose into cliffs almost a hundred feet high. The cliffs curved and bent the river into a lakelike lagoon extending over 300 feet to the south of the island. The St. Croix River disappeared from his view around the bend of the cliff, but he knew it joined the Mississippi River some fifty miles downstream.

Watching Rocky climb the boulders, he cupped his hands around his mouth and called. "Rocky, give me a hand with the gear, will you?"

Rocky called back. "Later, I'm busy."

Harvey headed down the path through the brush and stopped at the shore. "Come on, Rocky. I can't haul all that gear up the hill by myself. Let's get the tent up and our camp ready. Then we both can play."

"Listen!" Rocky stood on top of the boulders. He cocked his ear toward the high cliffs. "There's an echo. Hi!"

16

"Hi," the echo returned.

"There's an echo!" Rocky shouted.

"There's an echo," the echo returned.

Rocky shouted, sang, and yelled. The sound of his own voice coming back across the water filled him with a sense of power. He beat his chest with both fists and gave a Tarzan yell.

The yell returned. The echo sounded almost louder than Rocky.

Harvey got an idea. He faced the half-moon cliffs, cupped his hands and yelled out each word. He waited for the echo before sounding the next word.

"Rocky—*Rocky* . . . will—*will* . . . you—*you* . . . give—*give* . . . me—*me* . . . a—*a* . . . hand—*hand* . . . and—*and* . . . help—*help* . . . set—*set* . . . up—*up* . . . the—*the* . . . camp—camp."

Rocky looked annoyed. "I—*I* . . . will—*will* . . . not—*not.*" He turned to stare at Harvey.

Suddenly a voice came from the cliff. "Come on, Rocky. Give him a hand. Set up your camp."

Rocky almost fell from the boulder.

Harvey crouched against a rock.

17

Together their eyes searched the cliff to see from where the strange voice came. Then they saw a canoe at the base of the cliff.

A man was fishing in a small cove at the base of the cliff. He laughed and waved at the two boys.

Rocky flapped his hand in a weak reply. He crawled over the big boulders till he came to the shore. "Boy, for a solo campout, we sure do have a lot of people around."

At the beach, Rocky crammed his clothes back into the knapsack, slung it over his shoulder, and reached for the chest. Harvey grabbed the other handle. They carried the heavy chest up the hill. They were both panting when they dropped the box in the center of the clearing. Rocky sat on the box.

Harvey felt hot and removed his shirt. With each heave of his chest, his ribs showed through his thin but tanned skin. He folded his shirt and laid it on his knapsack. Comparing himself with Rocky's strong and husky body, he felt a little jealous. He sure wished he weighed more and had a better build. Then he smiled.

"Tell me, Rocky. Just how did you happen to fall in the river, anyway?"

Rocky looked up quickly. A hint of anger flicked across his face. Then he smiled and started to laugh.

"The rock moved." He laughed harder. "It was okay when I jumped out of the boat. But when I leaned forward to grab the boat, the rock moved. It pushed me against the boat, and the boat moved away. There I was. My feet on the rock, my hands on the boat and my butt up in the air. And that's when Mr. Adams turned. That's all it took. The boat moved some more and I had no place to go but down."

Harvey laughed. "You should have seen yourself when you came up. You were spitting water like a fountain."

"Yeah. Hurt my belly, too." He rubbed his stomach which still had a pink tint. "It's a good thing we had the rowboat instead of the canoe."

"Yeah. We'd all have been in the water." He motioned Rocky off the box and got the tent supplies. "I hung up your wet clothes."

Rocky shrugged. "Big deal."

2.
The Medal

As a team, they made camp. Harvey spread the ground cloth over the pine needles and Rocky buttoned together the two halves of the pup tent. They hung the tent over the two short poles which Harvey held while Rocky pounded in the stakes with the flat head of the axe.

"You know, if we do this right, we could win the prize as Best Campers," Harvey said with a trace of hope ringing in his voice. Now that Rocky was really helping, Harvey dared to tell him of his fondest wish.

"Us?" Rocky hooted. "Not on your life. You don't win prizes by having fun. And I expect to have fun."

"But we can try for the prize and still have fun."

Rocky stopped pounding stakes and sat back on his heels. He gave Harvey a long cool look. "I don't see how. To win prizes you have to do the job. And I don't care. You go for it if you want to, but leave me out. And don't give me any trouble."

Harvey didn't answer. He took a piece of rope and looped it over the front pole. Then he drove in a stake beyond the front of the tent and tied on the rope. He did the same with the back pole. Moving out from the tent, he carefully scanned the tent walls.

"Rocky, tighten up on that back rope, will you? Don't jerk it—now, straighten the pole—yes, the pole—there, that's fine."

Rocky scowled. "You see what I mean? That tent doesn't look any better to me now than it did before. Yet, all you want me to do is pull this, tighten that, straighten this. What fun is there to that?"

"But it looks better." Harvey took the shovel and began to dig a trench at the edge of the tent to catch any possible rain.

"How about getting some firewood, Rocky?" he suggested. When no answer came, he looked around, but Rocky was gone. He checked inside the tent to make sure. He shrugged his shoulders and kept working on the trench.

The prize was a medal for each boy on the winning team. Harvey wanted to win the medal just for the simple fun of winning something.

Being small for his age, he always lost the games and contests that called for strength. When they chose up sides for baseball or football, he was always one of the last ones picked.

He wanted to win the medal for a second reason. The kids on his block and at his school in the south side of Chicago never got to go camping. In fact, this was his first time camping, and it had only happened because his Uncle Leon had paid the bill. Yes, of course, he wanted the medal to show his

uncle, but even more, he wanted it to show the kids. He wanted to tell them about the fun of swimming in a clear, cool river, to tell them what it was like to fish from a canoe, then to clean the fish on the banks of the river, and finally to fry them to a golden brown over an open fire.

Harvey stood up. The trench seemed okay. When it rained, the water would drain away from the tent. Now he could finish his other jobs.

On the north side of the rocks that made the fire pit, he dug a hole for a garbage pit. Part way down the path on the left side, he found a group of bushes that made a half-circle. In the center of the circle, he dug a slit trench for a toilet. He stuck the shovel in the pile of dirt so that they could use it when needed. He placed a flat rock by the trench. From the storage box, he removed the toilet paper and the roll of plastic wrap. He covered the toilet paper with the plastic film and placed it on the rock.

Back at the fire pit, he found some flat rocks and arranged them in a pattern of small tables. With a hatchet, he chopped dead twigs and sticks from the trees for kindling. Then he piled up dead branches cut to the right length for his fire pit.

When finished, he looked over each part of the camp. He felt good. The camp looked neat. He knew he hadn't won any points, because there was nobody but himself to inspect the camp. But he didn't care.

Again, he looked around for Rocky, but couldn't see him anywhere. "Rocky! Rocky!" he called, but there was no answer. A hint of fear gripped his heart as he ran down the path to the south end of the island. He climbed the boulders and looked into the large holes that were like small caves. Rocky wasn't in any of them.

Shielding his eyes from the low afternoon sun, he searched each square foot of the river. He saw twigs and logs floating, but nothing that looked like a boy.

His mouth felt dry. Where had Rocky gone? What should he do?

"Rocky!" He yelled as loud as he could.

"Rocky," the echo replied.

25

Harvey was scared. His heart pounded. He ran around the small island and stopped again at the boulders. Rocky wasn't anywhere. He had disappeared.

Slowly, he trudged up the path to the camp. He removed the walkie-talkie from the box and just held it, looking at it.

This radio linked him with the base camp. They had to call once every morning and once in the evening to let Mr. Adams know that they were all right. In case of trouble, they could call in at anytime. Mr. Adams had said again and again that he didn't want anybody sick, hurt, or lost. Lost!

That was it! Rocky was lost!

Harvey knew he wasn't on the island. He refused to think of him floating face down in the river. He just had to be lost. He had to call for help even if it meant that would be the end of his three days.

He raised the antenna, turned on the switch, and brought the walkie-talkie to his lips. He took a deep breath, paused, thought again, but knew he had no choice. He pressed the speak button.

"Base Camp. This is Team Ten. Come in, please. Over."

He released the speak button. All he heard was static. He aimed the antenna toward the base camp and repeated.

"Base Camp. This is Team Ten. Come in, please, Over."

"Harvey! Harvey! What are you doing?"

Harvey turned. Rocky stood on the Minnesota shore waving his arms.

The radio sputtered. "Team Ten. This is Base Camp. What's the matter? Over."

Harvey pressed the speak button.

"Base Camp. This is Team Ten. Checking in for the night. Over."

"Checking in for the night?" the voice sounded startled. "Team Ten, you are supposed to call in around sundown. That's almost two hours away. Are you sure everything is all right? Over."

"Yeah. We're okay. Got our camp all set up and getting ready for dinner. Over."

"Okay. I'll put you down for your check-in. Next time, call at sundown. Over and out."

Harvey turned off the radio.

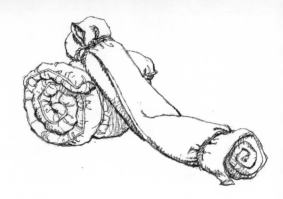

3.

A Woodsy Flavor

Harvey's legs trembled as he stood on the crest of the hill watching Rocky wade the shallow stream. Although he was glad to see him, glad to know that he wasn't lost or hadn't drowned, he was mad.

Rocky grabbed his towel from the wash line and dried himself as he came up the hill.

"What were you doing?"

Harvey scowled. "I thought you were lost."

"Me? Lost? What made you think that?"

"You weren't on the island. I looked all over for you. What did you expect me to do? You might have been drowned. How could I know? Don't go off again without telling me."

"Sure, Harvey. No need to get mad. Only you were so busy. I didn't know how shallow the water was."

"Where were you anyway?" Harvey asked.

"Just looking around." He wrapped the towel around his wet bathing suit and sat on the box. "I found Team Six. They're camping just around the bend up the river. What do you say we raid them tonight? Scare the blazes out of them."

"I think that's a crummy idea. It's time for dinner. I've done all the work so far. I think you should make dinner."

"Ha, ha. I'm telling you, Harvey. Team Six has the dumbest camp. I was just about to pounce on them when I heard you hollering. I knew I had to get back before you blew it. But how about it? Let's raid them tonight."

Harvey shook his head.

"But don't you see? You want to win the prize, don't you?"

Harvey's eyes brightened.

"If we raid them tonight, we can scare them. They might run back to base camp. Then there's one less team in the contest."

"That's a stupid idea," said Harvey. "If we were caught, we'd lose. And who wants to win by cheating?"

"Harvey, you sure are a big nothing. You just don't know how to have any fun. How about us? What if Team Six raids us? They know we're on this island. Bah!"

Harvey rubbed his stomach. "I'm hungry. I don't care about your stupid raid. Who makes dinner? You or me?"

Rocky grinned. "I'll cook. You clean up."

"Okay. We'll take turns on each meal. I'm going to lie down. Call me when it's ready."

Harvey put his gear in the pup tent. He unrolled his three-blanket bedroll. The other kids had razzed him for not having a sleeping bag. He couldn't help it if his parents couldn't buy him a sleeping bag.

He looked at Rocky's mummy sleeping bag. That was just the kind he would like to have.

Then he remembered Rocky's reputation for being a lousy cook. He could ruin all the food for their three days just by making one meal. Quickly he crawled from the tent and went to the fire pit. He shook his head. Boxes of food were tossed about. Tops were off bottles. A real mess. He began to pick things up. "What are you making?" he asked.

"Beans and hot dogs. We'll have to use pancakes as buns. That stupid Mr. Adams wouldn't let us have any bread."

Rocky bent over to blow on the coals. The burning sticks crackled and spit. Smoke and soot covered the pans.

"Why don't you get rid of the ashes in the beans?" Harvey asked.

Rocky shrugged. He picked up a spoon from the ground.

Harvey's mouth dropped open. He shouted. "Not with that! Don't you have any sense at all? Use a clean spoon!"

Rocky grunted and brushed the spoon against his trunks.

Harvey took a clean spoon from the box. His eyes almost popped. "Just look at your hands! They're filthy. Don't you know you can make us sick? Real sick. Go wash your hands."

Rocky's face twisted as if he had been slapped. "What?"

"I said go wash your hands. Now!" He reached into the box and picked up a bar of soap.

31

Rocky shook his head and moaned as he slowly stood up. "I'm camping with my mother. I just can't believe it. I'm camping with my mother." Taking the soap and his towel, he headed for the river.

Harvey scooped the ashes out of the beans. He added more water to the pancake batter because a thinner pancake would hold a hot dog easier. From the ice chest he took the butter, cut a pat and smeared the frying pan.

Rocky dropped the soap and towel on the box and flipped his hands in front of Harvey. "Okay? Do I pass now?"

Harvey nodded.

Rocky grabbed the frying pan. "You make me sick. You just don't know how to have any fun. Ashes won't kill you. It's just carbon. It adds flavor." He poured the pancake batter into the frying pan. "Put some wood on the fire. If I do it, I'll get my hands dirty. If I get my hands dirty, *you* might get sick."

"You don't need any more wood. Don't you know that hot coals cook better? What have you been doing this past month, just having fun?"

Rocky slammed the frying pan onto the logs. The sparks flew. He jumped up and shoved Harvey to the dirt. "I told you. Don't tell me what to do. Nag, nag, nag. Just shut your big mouth. I'm making this meal. You don't have to eat it."

Harvey blinked. He rose, brushed himself off, and picked up the soap. He got his towel and picked up the pail to fill for wash water.

Rocky squatted by the fire. He couldn't believe his eyes. The pancakes were covered with ashes. He tried scraping them off, but the ashes were baked into the pancakes. He flipped the pancakes out into the fire. Adding new batter to the frying pan, he started again. From the pot of beans, he scooped and scooped to get out the ashes.

Harvey saw the pancakes charring in the fire but said nothing.

Rocky tried to turn the new pancakes over. They were stuck to the pan. His knife dug and tore the half-cooked pancakes.

Harvey opened his mouth but then closed it. Going into the woods, he cut and trimmed a stick to use for toasting his hot dog. He cleaned the stick and cut a sharp point. After pushing on the hot dog, he held it over the fire.

Rocky still struggled with the pancakes. They were burnt, ripped, torn, and in shreds. He held the pan toward Harvey. "Pancakes?"

34

Harvey sneered. "I've seen garbage that looked better."

"Shut up. It's not my fault they won't let us have bread."

"All you had to do was put some butter in the pan. Then they wouldn't stick."

Rocky cut a small piece of pancake and tasted it. He spit it into the fire. "Yuck! Tastes as bad as it looks." Again he scraped them into the fire.

Harvey dripped some ketchup on his hot dog and ate it. He added a second one and held it over the fire.

Rocky spooned the beans into his plate. They had cooked so long they had become a soft dry mush that clung to his mouth like dry peanut butter. He worked his tongue against the mass to spit them into the fire.

"I don't think I want any beans, either."

Harvey ate his second hot dog and handed the stick to Rocky. Taking the pot of beans, he added water and stirred the dry mass. He spooned some into his plate and tasted them.

"Good. Needs a touch of salt." Tasting the beans again, he smacked his lips. "Just right,

Rocky. Like you said. The soot adds flavor. These are real smoked beans." He smacked his lips again. "You really should try these beans."

Rocky looked surprised. He spooned the beans into his plate and added some salt. The watery mass steamed in his plate. He tasted them. He spit the beans into the fire. Grabbing his canteen, he rinsed his mouth.

Harvey pretended not to see.

Rocky spat. "Bah! They're horrible. Like eating burnt wood."

"But the flavor. It's so woodsy."

"I think they're horrible. You eat them if you like them so much."

Harvey stood over Rocky. "Well, if you really want to know, I think they're horrible too." He tipped his plate so that the watery beans poured off and dripped onto Rocky's bare back.

Rocky jerked. His hot dog fell into the fire. He lunged for Harvey.

Harvey laughed as he jumped out of reach. "Next time, don't shove me around." He sped up the hill and hid in the brush.

36

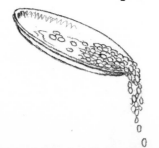

4.
Nag, Nag, Nag

Harvey waited until Rocky went for a swim to wash away the beans. Then he returned to the camp. He dumped the uneaten food into the garbage pit and kicked in a layer of dirt. Tossing the dirty dishes into the pail of hot water, he scrubbed them with a pad of steel wool until they glowed.

With the setting sun the wind seemed to blow harder. The yellow-and-red-tinged clouds scudded across the sky. Harvey added more wood to the fire.

Still feeling chilly, he went to the tent for his flannel shirt. Then he pulled the bag of marshmallows from the box. He looked down the hill at the water and called.

"Better come in, Rocky. It's getting late."

Rocky wouldn't answer.

Harvey held up the bag. "Let's toast some marshmallows." He turned to the fire, poured some water into the coffee pot and set it on the logs to heat. He recleaned the hot dog stick and pushed on a marshmallow.

Rocky came up the hill, drying himself off, and went in the tent to dress. When he came to the fire, he grabbed the marshmallows and popped one into his mouth. "Guess we're even," he mumbled.

Harvey grinned. "Guess we are. Want some hot chocolate? I'm heating the water."

"Great. With my dinner in the fire, I've got to eat something."

Harvey made the chocolate and handed a cup to Rocky.

"Thanks." He took a sip. "Good. But now, how about it? Are we going to raid Team Six?"

Harvey sat on the ground watching the flames char his marshmallow. He shook his head. "I think it's a stupid idea."

Rocky laughed. "I'm beginning to think you're a sissy. Where's your guts, anyway?"

Harvey shrugged. "I don't see any point in beating somebody up. Maybe it's because I've been beat up too many times myself."

"Look, we don't have to beat them up. Just scare them. We creep up real quiet, see. You from one side and me from the other. We make weird sounds. You hoot like an owl, maybe, while I do a wolf call. We just scare them, see. Oh, maybe, we toss a clod of dirt or two, but that's all. Then we sneak away. They'll never know who it was. Okay?"

Harvey began to grin. "You make it sound like fun, but it's not for me. I'm tired and I'm going to bed. There's too much to do tomorrow."

"Bah. You're no fun. And what's to do tomorrow? Just lie around a stupid island."

"There's plenty to do. We can improve our camp. Lash together some branches to make chairs. Lay out some paths. Go exploring."

Rocky picked up the water bucket and sprinkled the fire to put it out. "That sounds like work. Boy, somewhere I must have done something wrong. I can't understand how I let Mr. Adams stick me with you. I know why nobody from your tent would go with you."

Harvey stopped. "You do?" He felt his stomach twitch. It had bothered him that the other four boys in his tent had all paired off for the three-day test to leave him as a loner to be paired off with another loner from the other tents. "Why?"

"Because you're a know-it-all. Just like my mother. A know-it-all. Can't be happy unless you're always working. Don't know how to relax and have fun. Boy, if I can last three days with you, I'll be doing good, real good."

Harvey didn't answer. He crawled into the tent and lit the candle in the cut can that was their lantern.

He pulled his flannel pajamas and slipper socks from his knapsack and changed clothes. Sliding between his covers, he leaned back with his hands behind his head. His eyes stared at the lights and shadows dancing across the top of the tent.

Rocky crawled in, slipped off his shoes and squirmed his way into his mummy-shaped sleeping bag. He jerked the zipper from where it was stuck to close up more of the bag. Sitting up, he munched on some more of the marshmallows.

"You shouldn't have brought food into the tent," Harvey complained.

"And another reason nobody wants to camp with you is that you always nag. You're always complaining. You know that?"

Harvey cringed from the attack. "I'm sorry, Rocky. I don't mean to nag. It's just that— It's just that I've had to take care of my younger brother and sister so much, I guess.

41

I'm just looking out for the other guy. My mom works in the afternoons as often as she can. Then I'm in charge of the house. If anything goes wrong, I'm the one that gets the blame."

The anger left Rocky's voice. "Well, just remember, I'm not your brother or sister and you're not in charge of me."

"I know that."

Rocky rolled up the bag of marshmallows and propped it at the edge of the tent. He punched his knapsack into shape and used it as a pillow. "Sometimes I wish my mother worked. She's always home. Always telling me what to do."

Harvey nodded.

"What does your dad do anyway, Harvey?"

"He's an office manager for a finance company."

"My dad is sales manager for a farm machinery factory. He's gone a lot. He travels all the farm states."

"Gee, that sounds like a good job."

"I guess it is. But he's gone a lot. He promised to take me hunting this fall. Deer hunting. Up north, near the Canadian border. I like to hunt."

Harvey's eyes opened wide. "I've never been hunting. No chance in a big city like Chicago. I go to the park a lot. But you can't hunt in the park."

"My dad gets a deer every year. He knows where to go. He took my brother last year. I guess he'll take him again this year. They both got a deer last year."

"Gee. I'd like to go deer hunting."

"Me, too. All I've done so far is hunt rabbits. I got a twenty-two for my birthday last year. A single shot. It's hard hitting rabbits with a single shot. I want a repeater. Maybe I'll get it this year."

"Yeah. Boy, I'd be happy with a single shot. Gee, you sure are lucky, Rocky."

Rocky sat up with a jerk. The mummy cowl dropped from his head. "What's that?"

Harvey sat up and leaned on his elbow. He whispered, "What's what?"

"That noise. Hear it? That moaning noise?"

Harvey held his breath, closed his eyes and strained his ears.

The moan sounded low like a waving sigh of despair. "I hear it." The cold fingers of fear clutched his heart.

"What is it?"

In slow motion, Harvey quietly slipped from his blankets, picked up his flashlight, and poked his head out the front of the tent. He flashed the light around the camp, then crawled out from the tent. The moan stopped.

Rocky's head jutted from the tent. "What is it?"

"I don't know. I don't see anything. Guess it must have been the wind."

Rocky crawled from the tent. His light flashed through the trees and brush. "The wind seems to have stopped."

"And so has the moan. It must have been the wind." Harvey shuddered. "There's nothing here. I'm getting cold."

The boys crawled back into the tent.

Back in his blanket Harvey listened hard. He didn't hear the moan. "I guess it was the wind. Blow out the candle. Let's go to sleep."

In the dark Harvey still listened. Soon his eyes closed and he fell asleep.

5.

Checking In

Harvey heard the birds chirping as the morning sun peeped under the edge of the tent. It took him a moment to remember where he was. He looked at Rocky, who was still fast asleep. Quietly, he put on his clothes and crawled from the tent.

The air smelled fresh and clean. The squirrels and chipmunks were busy searching for food. When they saw Harvey, they scurried from the camp to hide in the forest.

Harvey turned on the walkie-talkie and heard nothing but static. He figured it might be too early to check in, so he started breakfast.

He built a small fire and began to fry the bacon. The tangy smell made his mouth water. He was hungry. He took the eggs from the ice chest. When he heard a noise, he turned.

Rocky stood behind him putting on his sweater. "I guess I'll have some breakfast, too. I'm starved after that lousy supper last night."

Harvey smiled. He added two more bacon slices. When crisp, he lifted each strip to let the hot grease drip back into the pan. He set the bacon on a plate and poured most of the grease into the fire. The fire snapped and flared from the new fuel. The smell of bacon grease filled the air.

"Fried or scrambled?"

"Scrambled." Rocky reached over and took one of the hot bacon slices. Even though it burned his mouth, he nibbled on it.

Harvey beat the eggs in a cup, poured them into the hot pan and stirred them until they were cooked. He salted the eggs and divided them between their two plates.

"Too bad we don't have some cheese. I like my eggs with cheese. Maybe when we're back at base camp, you could join me for a cheese omelet breakfast. It's very good."

47

Rocky looked at Harvey in a funny way. "You'll have me for breakfast?"

"Sure. Why not? That is if you want to. I've done most of the cooking for my tent during the past month. The other four guys in my tent cook worse than you do. That meal you made last night was almost a feast compared to what they make."

A faint blush tinged Rocky's face. "Well, I've never cared about cooking—except for fish, that is. Our tent ate okay, I guess. Not real good, you know, but okay."

Harvey nodded as he finished his eggs.

"Sure, Harvey. I've heard you cook real good. I'll be glad to join you for breakfast. What can I lose?"

Harvey felt pleased. Maybe this three-day campout would be more fun than he had expected. Rocky wasn't such a bad guy after all. "I'll clean up while you fix up the tent." He threw the dirty dishes into the pail of hot water.

"Let's call in first." Rocky picked up the walkie-talkie. All he heard was static. "Think we should call in?"

"I don't care. Just so we aren't the ones who wake them up, that's all."

Just then the radio sputtered into sound. But the words didn't come through loud enough. Then, "Team Eight. This is Base Camp. Over."

They couldn't hear the message from Team Eight, who were camping far up the river. They were out of range of the small walkie-talkie.

"Team Eight. This is Base Camp. Check in this evening. Over and out."

Harvey nodded. "Team Eight is from my tent. They should do pretty good. How did the guys in your tent pair off?"

"They made Teams Two and Seven. I figure Team Seven will fold, but Team Two should make the three days all right. What was the other team from your tent?"

Harvey smiled. "Three. Team Three. Just a couple of kids. I don't think they'll last." Harvey stacked the cleaned dishes on the rocks. "Okay, Rocky, why don't you check in now?"

Before Rocky could push the speak button,

the radio crackled into sound again. "Base Camp. This is Team Three. Over."

Harvey stood up. "That's them, Rocky. The kids I was just telling you about."

"Team Three. This is Base Camp. Over."

"Base Camp. We've had some trouble. Over." The young voice almost broke into tears.

"See. I told you." Harvey moved next to Rocky.

"What kind of trouble? Over."

"We don't know. Our food box has been tipped over and all the stuff messed up."

The voice of Mr. Adams came over the radio. "Team Three, this is Mr. Adams. What happened? Do you see any tracks or footprints? Over."

"There are tracks. They look like dog tracks or wolf tracks. We can't be sure. All we know is that we don't have anything to eat and we're hungry. Over."

"Okay, Team Three. Take it easy. We'll have someone there in a few minutes. Just get your gear ready. Over and out."

"Over and out."

The static continued. Rocky grinned. "Sounds like they fold. One down and nine to go. Maybe we should listen to all the calls. That way we'd know what's going on."

"Yeah. But it would wear out the battery."

"So?"

"Well, I'm not really surprised about Team Three. They were the youngest kids. They must have left their food out and some dog got it."

"Or a wolf."

Harvey shook his head. "Naw. I don't think there are really any wolves around here. I think that's just some made-up stories to scare us. Why don't you call in now?"

Rocky pushed the speak button. "Base Camp. This is Team Ten. Over."

"Team Ten. This is Base Camp. Over."

"Team Ten checking in. Everything running smooth and easy. Over."

"Fine, Team Ten. Check in tonight. Over and Out."

"Over and out." Rocky turned the radio off. "How'd you like that? Everything smooth and easy."

"Well, you tell it just like it is, Rocky."

Harvey cleaned up the camp while Rocky went off to fish. Stripping branches of twigs, Harvey lashed the branches to make himself a chair. He started a second chair for Rocky. It felt good using last month's training.

"Fish just aren't biting," Rocky snorted when he came back. He dropped the fishing gear at the box. "Say, they look pretty good." He pulled the chair over and tried it out. "Sure does beat sitting on a rock."

"Yeah. That's what I thought too."

Rocky stood up and patted his pockets. "Can you loan me a quarter?"

Harvey looked surprised. "What do you want a quarter for?"

"I just want a quarter. I'll pay you back when we get to base camp."

Harvey shook his head as he reached into his pocket. "Doesn't make any sense to me. There's no place to use money on this island."

Rocky shrugged. "Thought maybe I'd hike to the store and get me some candy. That dumb Mr. Adams wouldn't let us bring any with us."

Harvey stood up. "But that's just the idea, Rocky. We're supposed to live off just what we brought. If we need anything else we have to get it from the land or the river."

"Well—the way I look at it is—the store is on the land, so that's living off the land."

Harvey scowled. "It isn't right. You're twisting words."

"So what."

Rocky put on his bathing suit and waded the stream to the Minnesota shore. Harvey shook his head as Rocky disappeared into the trees.

When he finished with the chair, he picked up the fishing rod and went to the river bank. Lying on his back, he watched the lazy clouds drift across the deep blue sky. He felt peaceful and happy.

The water bubbled past the bank, and his line drifted back and forth as the current moved his float. But he had no bites or nibbles. Either the fish weren't biting or he was in the wrong spot.

Returning to the camp, he decided to take a nap. He had done enough for the morning.

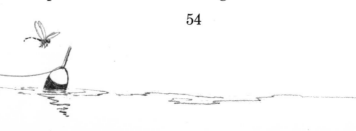

6.
Wilted Lettuce

Harvey woke in mid-afternoon in the hot tent. Although he had kicked off most of his covers, beads of sweat coated his face. His back felt wet against the blankets. He felt hot, dirty, and sweaty.

Rocky was also asleep, so Harvey crawled out of the tent. He padded down the path to the latrine. When he was finished, he re-wrapped the toilet paper in the plastic film and shoveled a layer of dirt in the trench.

Taking his soap and towel, he headed for the river and a fast bath. Then he paddled and floated in the cool water of the shallow stream waiting for Rocky to wake up.

He watched the dragonflies dart over the water. At times he heard the splash of a frog. The river seemed to steam in the August sun.

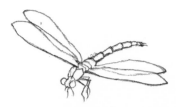

Next week, Harvey would be back home in South Chicago, and he was a little sorry. The long summer was coming to an end. He had learned a lot and had had a lot of fun during this month of survival training. He wished he could stay, because this was really living.

His stomach grumbled. He decided to get dinner started early since he had slept through lunch. He dried, dressed, and returned to camp to build a fire.

Rocky crawled out of the tent and paused by a bush.

Harvey got mad. "Rocky! What are you doing?"

"I'm watering a bush."

"But we have a place for that. Do you want to stink up the whole camp? Don't you have any sense at all?"

"Aw, shut up. When will you learn that camping is getting back to nature?"

"So? It might be getting back to nature, but that doesn't mean that we become animals. Boy! I have a dog at home that has better habits than you do."

Rocky stomped over to the storage box.

"I'm hungry. What are we going to eat? All the ice is gone. Guess we better clear out the ice chest."

"No you don't." Harvey bounded over. "I'll do it. I don't want your filthy hands pawing the food. Why don't you wash up. You stink."

"You stink too."

"Not now. I took a bath. I woke before you did and took a bath so I wouldn't stink."

"But you do stink, Harvey. You stink of rules and orders—with your nag, nag, nag!"

"Don't be an idiot. All I said was for you to wash up. That's not nagging. It's just good sense. You should have done it without being told. I don't understand you. You don't know the first thing about good health. Didn't your mother ever teach you anything? Now, I'll take care of the food. You go wash up."

Rocky shook his head. "I'm camping with my mother. I'm camping with my mother." He trudged to the river.

Harvey wrapped two potatoes in aluminum foil and buried them in the hot coals of the fire. Since they took the longest to cook, he started them first.

He decided they would have a feast since they were combining two meals into one. He put all the salad items into a big pot, the hamburger on a dish. The box of biscuit mix would make the buns for the hamburgers.

With the aluminum foil, he built a reflector oven at the side of the fire so that he could bake the biscuit patties. He dumped the biscuit mix in a bowl, added water, and stirred. Melting some butter, he added it to the biscuit mix. His mother always did this, and her biscuits were delicious. He dusted his hands with the dry biscuit mix, pulled some batter from the bowl, and patted the dough into a large thin disk. He made four disks which he slid into the oven.

He had all the fixings for a salad, but no salad dressing. He decided to make his mother's favorite, wilted lettuce salad. He put the last of the bacon in the pan and set it on the fire. Removing the outer leaves from the small head of lettuce, he cut the lettuce into cubes. He peeled a large brown onion and diced it. The lettuce and onion went into the bowl.

58

He sliced the tomatoes into wedges and the carrots into strips and set them on a plate. Crumpling the crisp bacon into the bowl, he poured in the bacon grease and stirred. The lettuce became slippery and shiny as the grease coated the leaves. He added several pickle slices along with some pickle juice from the jar. Scooping the salad into two bowls, he added the carrot strips, tomato wedges and a few olives.

"Salad's ready."

"I don't like salad," Rocky grumbled as he took it.

"Try it. You might like it. Has a strong bacon flavor."

Harvey tasted his salad. It had a good, strong, tangy bacon flavor. The tart acid from the pickle juice tickled his tongue. He was pleased.

Rocky ate a tomato wedge and then the olives and carrots. He speared the lettuce, tasted, and smacked his lips. "Say, Harvey, this is good. I've never had salad as good as this before."

Harvey smiled. "I think you're hungry.

Anything tastes good when you're hungry."
He jabbed his fork into the two potatoes.
They were almost cooked. He turned the biscuits in his little oven to get an even brown-
ing. Placing the hamburger patties into the
frying pan, he dusted them with salt and
pepper.

When they were cooked, he spread mustard
and pickles on one biscuit, added the hamburger and the second biscuit. He gave it to
Rocky and made another for himself.

He scooped the potatoes from the coals and
put one on Rocky's plate. He sliced his own
potato, pushed the ends to open it up, and
spread the butter over the center.

Rocky was bug-eyed. "I've never tasted
chow this good all summer. How do you do
it?"

Harvey wiped a trickle of butter from his
chin. "Well, it takes time. Baked potato must
be cooked. Most people on a campout don't
give them enough time to get done."

"Sure. But you must have cooked before.
You didn't learn all this during the past
month."

Harvey nodded. "My dad likes to cook—out in the back yard. He's shown me a lot."

"You know what, Harvey? I think this is the first time in the last month that I'm not hungry."

Harvey smiled. He was glad that Rocky liked the feast.

7.

Friends

The sun was setting. Harvey and Rocky lay on their stomachs watching the orange, red, and yellow flames of their campfire dance in the breeze. The wood spit and crackled when the heat exploded the sap and turned it to steam.

Rocky threw more wood on the fire and poked the coals. Glowing sparks whipped through the air to dart through the tree branches.

"Be careful, Rocky. With the wind blowing the way it is, you don't know where those sparks will land. We don't want to start a forest fire."

He rose and went to the tent to get his sweater. Looking at the sky, he saw the fast-moving clouds gliding across the light of the moon. They sent eerie shadows stalking across the surface of the river. A chilly north wind rippled the surface of the water, and the pine trees waved back and forth. Now and then a stronger gust of wind blasted the island to whip the brush into wild motion.

Harvey returned to the campfire, pulled his chair close, and sat down. "Looks like a storm is coming."

"So? Who cares? I was just thinking that next week I'll be back in Minneapolis and have to put up with my stupid brother again."

Harvey nodded. "How old is he?"

"Dick? He's sixteen. He's a big star in football. He's got a motorcycle—a scrambler."

"Boy, I'd like to have a scrambler. Does he take you for rides?"

"Sometimes. But most of the time he makes my life miserable. He's always calling me sissy."

Harvey looked surprised. "Sissy? What do you mean?"

"It's my lousy name. That's why I hate school. They always call you by your real name. I hate my name. That's why I like

Rocky. It's the only good thing I can make with my stupid name."

"I never thought about it. To me you were always Rocky."

"And that's the way I like it. My last name is Rockford. My stupid parents named me after my uncles."

"They did? Mine did too. I'm Harvey Leon. Harvey is my mother's brother and Leon is my father's brother. In fact, I'm only here because of my Uncle Leon. He paid my way so I could take this survival training." He waited, then asked "What is your real name anyway?"

Rocky made a sour face. "If I tell you, everybody in the camp will know. I'd be ruined for sure. I've told you too much already."

"Aw, Rocky, don't be an idiot. I won't tell, I promise."

"I've heard promises before. Naw, I'm not telling you."

"But I promise, Rocky. Swear on a Bible, or a bloody cat. How's that? An oath, signed in blood."

Rocky squirmed. He leaned his head close to Harvey. "Okay. But if I find you talking, you'll have a bloody cat all right. I'll smash your nose in. That's what."

"I won't tell."

"It's Cecil."

"Cecil?" Harvey tried not to smile.

"Yeah. Horrible, isn't it. And my stupid brother makes it worse. He calls me C-C and says 'Sissy.'"

"Yeah. I'd hate to have a cruddy name like that. Why don't you use your middle name?"

"Yuck. That's Melvin. And you should hear how my big ape brother makes a big deal of that. Naw. I've got a lousy name."

Harvey thought a few minutes. "I've got an idea, Rocky. There's a big football player. I'm sure he's with the Chicago Bears. He's got a terrible name."

"So?"

"What he does is just use his initials. O. J., I think it is. Or C. J. It's one or the other."

"Yeah." Rocky's eyes brightened. "C. M. I see what you mean. C. M. That doesn't sound too bad, does it?"

"No, C. M. It doesn't. And you know what?
"What?"

"What it stands for. C. M. Concrete Mixer. Concrete Mixer Rockford, called Rocky for short." Harvey grinned.

"C. M. Concrete Mixer. C. M. You know, Harvey, I think you've got something there. C. M. I like it."

"You want me to call you C. M.?"

"Oh, Rocky's all right."

"I know, Rocky. But it might give you a chance to get used to it. Really see if you want to be called C. M. or not."

"Okay, Harvey. Sure, call me C. M."

Rocky rose, brushed the dirt off his shirt and pulled his chair over. The wind tossed his hair into a churning mass.

"What grade are you in, C. M.?"

Rocky looked at Harvey. He was having a little trouble getting used to his new name. "Me? I start sixth grade next month. What about you?"

"I start eighth grade this year."

"You do? What are you, a brain?"

"Not really. I study a lot. I don't have

much else to do. I don't go out for sports because I can never make the team."

"Why don't you exercise? Build up your muscles."

"I do."

"You do? What kind?"

"Breathing exercises. Every morning and evening for fifteen minutes."

"What do you do that for?"

"I'm trying to build my wind. I'm in the band."

"You are!" Rocky looked interested. "What do you play?"

"The tuba."

Rocky shook his head. "I don't believe it. The tuba. That's a big thing, isn't it?"

"Yes, C. M. That's why I like it. It's the biggest horn and plays loud. I've got the loudest horn in the band."

"Well, I think you're stupid, Harvey. Play the tuba if that's what you want. But if you want to build your wind, go out for track."

"I'd never make the team."

"Boy! You know you might be smart with books, but I think you're pretty dumb. Track isn't a team sport. I'm telling you, Harvey, track will build your wind."

"You know, C. M., I've never really thought about it. Maybe I will go out for track when school starts. I sure would like to do something. How about you? I'll bet you do good in football."

"Yeah. In a way I do. My brother's helped me a lot. I think I'm better than he is. But my trouble is that nobody wants to play with me. I'm too big for the kids in my class. They're afraid of me. That's why I hunt so much. I don't need anybody to have fun hunting. Just me. Me against the world."

"I know. I get that feeling too. That's when I go to the music room and blow on my tuba. It makes me happy. I feel good. What do you do to feel good?"

"How can I feel good? Anytime I try something, my brother chops me down. If I win something, everybody says it's because I'm big. How does a guy feel good?"

"Well, like I said. I do it with the tuba. Do you have something like that? Something all your own?"

"Well, I guess I do," admitted Rocky.

"Fine. What is it?"

"You won't laugh, will you?"

"Of course not."

"And promise—you won't tell anybody."

"Of course, C. M. What is it?"

"Well, I like to draw cartoons. I'm pretty good at it. When I get real mad at my brother, I go to my room and make up some silly cartoons. That way I get to laugh at him. He's so stupid. In the cartoon I can show how stupid he is. And like at school—some of the teachers are pretty stupid. Not dumb, you know. Just stupid. Won't listen to you or won't try to understand. I put them in cartoons. I get to laugh at them, and I feel better. Yeah, Harvey, I see what you mean. You play the tuba, and I draw cartoons."

"Gee, I'd like to draw cartoons. Do you have any with you?"

"Here? You must be kidding. I don't want these guys thinking I'm a sissy artist. I only do them in my bedroom where I keep them in a box. Nobody sees them."

"I'd like to see them. Would you let me?"

Rocky hesitated. "Well, sure. But they're all at my house in Minneapolis."

"Well, when we get back to camp, maybe you could draw me one or two. We can go out in the woods where nobody else would know."

"Okay, Harvey. Yeah, I don't mind if you see them, I guess. Sure. I'll draw you some when we get back."

"Good." Harvey rose and looked upriver. "I'm so tired I can barely stand up. I'm going to bed before that storm hits. Put the fire out when you're through."

"Okay."

8.

The Storm

Harvey woke when something hit his leg. He bolted up. His head hit the wall of the tent.

"What. . .?"

"It's raining. Turn on your flashlight. I can't see. The rain started with no warning. All of a sudden, pow! There it was."

Harvey turned on his flashlight. The wind whipped through the tent and the walls flapped. He bent down to button the front flap. Time after time the wind tore the flaps from his grasp. When he buttoned the last button, he lay down again.

Rocky lit the tin-can candle lantern. The flame danced and flickered as the wind seethed through the cracks. The shadows jiggled across the tent walls.

Harvey turned off his flashlight. "What do

you need the candle for? Let's go to sleep."

"Not me. Not with this storm. I can't sleep." Rocky set the tin-can candle at the foot of his sleeping bag. He crossed his legs, propped his elbows on his knees, and gripped his chin between his fists.

The rain beat against the cover of trees and pounded through to pelt the canvas tent. Small spurts of water dripped through the holes in the old tent walls.

Outside, the wind whipped the river into a frenzy of whitecaps. The trees bent, twisted, and some snapped. The rain beat the trees, the brush, and the ground in a steady torrent. The lightning flashed and the thunder crashed. The ground grew soft and mushy as it sopped up the water. Small streams ripped across the island to pour into the river.

The tent shook and trembled as the wind hit the sides. With each gust, the tent tugged and pulled at the stakes, which strained against the soft waterlogged ground. The rain streamed down the walls of the tent to fill the ditch. The ditch overflowed, and water sloshed across the ground to run inside the tent.

Harvey shuddered, wondering how long the tent could hold out. He pulled his blankets around him and moved closer to the center of the tent. Wherever his head brushed the canvas, water oozed through the fabric.

"The water's flowing in."

"So what?" Rocky ducked the water dripping through the old tent wall. "It's all water. What's the difference if it flows in or pours in. This is just a lousy tent."

"I've never seen it rain so hard. Do you think we'll have a flood?"

"Naw. It's too late in the year. The floods come in the spring when all the snow melts."

"Has this island ever been flooded?"

"Of course. Every spring, like I said. But the river's too low to flood from just one rainstorm. Don't be so scared."

That's when it happened. It happened fast. It lasted only a few seconds. But to Harvey it seemed forever.

Lightning struck the island.

Harvey sensed a strange change in the air. He felt the hair on his head stand straight up. An eerie glow flooded the inside of the tent

for less than the wink of the eye. But the glow seared the eye so that the image lasted a much longer time. The glow left the tent in deep black darkness that even seemed to smother the light of the candle.

A strange odor filled the air.

And almost at the same time came the most scary part of all—a shattering, bone-shaking, overwhelming noise.

The noise started as a sharp, brittle snap like the crack of a rifle. Only much louder. A clean, distinct, brittle snap that repeated and grew.

The thunder rolled and rumbled. The sound boomed against the cliff to echo back and forth. Harvey pressed his hands over his ears to shut out the sound. He felt his body almost float in the air.

Slowly, his eyes recovered sight.

Rocky had fallen backward and seemed to be in a trance. The candle had fallen over and was burning the end of his sleeping bag.

"Look out!" Harvey bent down and beat out the flames with his hands. "You okay? Rocky?"

"What happened?" Rocky seemed dazed.

"Lightning. I think the island was hit by lightning."

The wind ripped through the tent. It blasted the stakes from the soft ground. Suddenly the tent shuddered, pulled loose, and sailed through the air.

The torrent of rain fell on the two boys. It drenched their blankets and soaked their clothes.

"What are we going to do?" Rocky shouted.

"We can't stay here. That's for sure."

"How about the rocks? The caves in the rocks."

"Yeah, at least we can keep the wind off. Let's go. Grab the ground cloth."

"What for? It's all wet."

"So what. Isn't everything? Take it. If we don't, it will just blow away."

Rocky struggled out of his mummy bag, grabbed the ground cloth, and ran down the hill to the boulders.

Harvey followed. He felt the water soaking his slipper socks and the rain pelting his back.

Reaching the boulders, they squeezed their

77

way into a small cave made by a circle of boulders. The wind and rain blew through the many cracks and openings. Streams of water cut across the floor of the cave. But the rocks did cut down on the force of the wind and on the amount of rain.

They wrapped themselves in their covers as best as they could. Rocky draped the ground cloth over his head and pinched it closed under his chin. Only his face peered out.

"Wow! This is a terrible storm. I've never seen it rain so hard."

"Me, neither." Harvey tucked his knees under his chin. He wrapped the blanket over his shoulders like a cape, with one corner resting over his head.

"Do you think we should call base camp, Harvey?"

"What for? Do you want to quit?"

"No. Of course not. But they might be worried. That lightning bolt could have killed us, you know."

"I'll bet they don't even know the island was hit. They are sitting in big tents. To them, one lightning bolt is just like another."

"Yeah, I guess you're right. Gee, I'm wet. This isn't any fun. I feel just plain miserable."

Harvey squirmed in the tight cave, trying to make more room for himself. "I'm miserable too. But I'm not ready to quit. The longer we last, the better our chances for winning the medal."

Rocky sneered. "Who cares about some stupid medal? Just move your feet, will you? My legs are cramped."

Harvey twisted in the cave to find a new position to sit. He pulled at the covers trying to find a dry place to lay across his shoulders.

Gradually the rain and wind lessened. Most of the lightning flashes were now downriver. They didn't have to shout as much anymore.

Harvey crawled from the cave. His back hurt where he had leaned against the rock. His legs were cramped and his feet tingled with numbness. He pulled his water-soaked blankets. The water squished from his socks. He rubbed his arms and legs to restore his circulation.

"I'm stiff," Rocky grumbled.

"I'm soaked. Let's get a fire started and dry out."

Harvey struggled up the hill to the camp. The wind had almost stopped, but the wet, muddy ground was slippery. For every two steps forward, he slid one step back. Behind him, he heard Rocky having the same trouble.

Finding the tin-can candle, he reached into

the pocket of his soaked pants for the vial of special matches. At the fire pit he lit the candle and set the candle down. Filling a metal cup with wet wood chips, he set it over the candle flame to dry.

"Get me some pots and more candles."

Rocky dropped his soggy sleeping bag. "And make some hot chocolate. I could use something warm."

Harvey flashed his light into the storage box. Everything was wet. Pawing over the dripping, limp boxes and bags, he shook his head.

He took out the aluminum foil and extra candle. At the fire he spread the foil on the wet ground and poured the cup of dried wood on the foil. He refilled the cup with more wet wood. Lighting the second candle, he dripped wax over the partly dried wood and finally used the candle flame to light the wax-soaked wood.

Harvey filled a pail with wet wood and hung the pail over the fire. He kept adding more twigs to the fire. He nursed and fed the blaze, building his stocks of dried wood. It was a long, slow process, but finally the small logs began to burn. The heat felt good against his cold damp skin.

He helped Rocky wring out the blankets and squeeze the mummy bag. Rocky strung a rope and hung them over the fire.

"Do you have any idea what time it is, Harvey?"

"No. But if the stars were out, I'd know."

"You would? You mean you can tell time from the stars? I thought you could only tell time from the sun."

"Works the same way with the stars, C. M. I've been watching the stars up here. I've never seen them so real and close. We hardly ever see the stars in Chicago. There is always too much light in the sky." He added more wood to the fire. "Did you ever wonder why the Indians had so many stories about the stars?"

Rocky looked puzzled. "Why make up stories about the stars? Who really cares?"

"I care. I like reading about them. The Indians told many stories about the stars. The only light they had at night was a campfire. They could really see the night sky. They could tell time and direction from the stars."

Rocky nodded. "Sure. But right now, I want to know what time it is. Maybe we should call the base camp and let them know we are okay."

"Good idea."

Rocky turned on the walkie-talkie. It popped and crackled from the static electricity in the air.

The radio sputtered. "—Come—in, please—"

The two boys looked at each other. The radio kept sputtering.

"Attention — all — all — teams — camp — is Base Camp—please. Come in—Over."

Rocky pushed the speak button. "Base Camp. This is Team Ten. Over."

"—Ten. This is —each—repeat—each sen— bad. Static is—over. Over."

"Give it here." Harvey snatched the radio. He spoke slowly and clearly. "Base Camp. Base Camp. This is Team Ten. This is Team Ten. Over. Over."

The radio crackled. "Team—Ten—right. Are you all—Over. Over."

"Team Ten is fine. Team Ten is fine. We are wet. We are wet. But we are fine. But we are fine. What time is it? What time is it? Over. Over."

"—Team—know you—glad to know— fine—two o'clock—time is—o'clock. Do— quit—you want to—Over."

"Team Ten won't quit. Team Ten won't quit. We are fine. We are fine. Over. Over."

"Over—out."

"Over and out. Over and out."

Rocky took the radio. "I think they're really worried, don't you? They're calling all teams at two o'clock in the morning."

"I guess so. But you know we could have been killed with that lightning bolt and all. I can't blame them for being worried."

"Yeah. We were lucky I guess. All we lost was that tent."

Harvey shook his head. "And our food. Our food is a mess."

Rocky felt his sleeping bag. "This thing is never going to dry. I can't put it any closer to the fire or it'll burn up. I already got one hole in it."

"Well, if you'll remember, I told you not to light the candle."

"Shut up, Harvey. Anything I hate is an 'I-told-you-so.' This is going to be a long, cold, wet night, and I don't need you nagging at me."

Harvey felt his blankets. Only the corner closest to the fire was getting dry.

"Is the water hot yet?" Rocky peered into the bubbling pot. "We'll have to make coffee. The cocoa box is soaked."

For hours they huddled over their fire, drying wood, moving blankets, and sipping coffee. As the morning sun gave a grey-yellow glow to the sky, Harvey had two blankets dry enough to use.

Rocky sighed. "Too bad I don't have my gun with me. We could hunt rabbit."

Harvey shrugged. "I'm too tired to think about it now. Take one of my blankets. It's still damp but it's better than nothing."

Rolling himself in the blanket, Harvey lay down on the ground cloth by the fire. In a flash he was asleep.

9.
Toilet Paper

Harvey rolled around in his blanket. He opened one eye to see the sun high in the sky. Hearing somebody calling him, he raised his head. Rocky's blanket lay on the ground. Again he heard his name called. He sat up.

"Yes? What do you want?"

"Do we have any paper?" Rocky's voice called.

"Any paper?" Harvey crawled from his blanket and stood up.

"Yes. Any paper. All the toilet paper is wet."

"You know we haven't any paper. Use leaves or something."

"I can't. Anyway, leaves scratch."

Harvey opened the storage box. There was no paper. He turned, holding up empty hands.

Rocky shrugged and slowly duck-walked across the clearing to the river. His bare bottom flapped against his heels. He washed himself in the stream.

Harvey picked up the soap and Rocky's towel and took them down to him.

"Guess I've got the runs."

"You should. The way you eat without ever washing up."

At the camp Harvey sadly shook his head as he looked in the storage box. The pancake batter was a soggy mass. So was the biscuit mix, cocoa, powdered milk, and the sugar. The jars of syrup, pickles, mustard, and the can of beef stew he stacked to one side. The dried soup packed in the aluminum foil looked all right. The fizzies also were okay. On the bottom of the box, he found a package of corn meal. Although the box was wet and soft, the metal-coated paper inside had kept the corn meal from getting wet.

"What's for breakfast?" Rocky threw his towel on top of his sleeping bag.

"Not much. If you want something fast, try a pickle."

"A pickle!" Rocky pawed over the wet boxes. "I'm starved. I need more than a pickle for breakfast."

"I know, I'm hungry too. All we've got is a can of beef stew and some soup."

"Yuck. Whoever heard of soup or stew for breakfast?"

"We're going to have to catch some fish, C. M. I think we should eat the stew. Then we can go fishing."

Rocky went to his sleeping bag for the radio.

"Base Camp. This is Team Ten. Come in, please. Over."

The radio crackled with a little static. "Team Ten. This is Base Camp. Good Morning. Over."

Rocky looked at Harvey. "Base Camp. Team Ten is fine. Our food got wet. Can we get some more food? Over."

"Team Ten. Any other damages? Over."

"We lost our tent. It blew away in the storm. We haven't been able to find it yet. Over."

"Do you want to quit? Over."

"Team Ten won't quit. What we want is more food. It's not our fault the storm ruined our food. Over."

"Team Ten. You know the rules. You make do with what you've got for another day or else you quit. If you want to quit, we'll have the boat at the island in half an hour. Over."

Rocky was angry. "Team Ten won't quit. Over and out."

"Hold it, Team Ten. You're sure you're both okay?"

"Yes. We're both okay. Just hungry. Over."

"Okay, Team Ten. Make out the best way you can. Live off the land. Catch some fish. Try and find that tent. If it gets too tough, call in anytime. We can pick you up. Over."

"Over and out."

"Over and out."

"Pass me the pickles." Rocky put the radio back, opened the jar of pickles and took a plump one to munch. His mouth puckered from the biting acid.

"Look, C. M. I'll get the stew started. You go find the tent. Then we'll get the fishing stuff together. Let's try to catch some fish."

"Bah. If they weren't watching that stupid store, I'd go buy some food."

"Huh? What'd you say?"

Rocky fumbled in his pocket and threw Harvey the quarter. "They have one of the adult leaders watching the store. I was lucky yesterday. I saw him talking to the guys from Team Four. He had caught them coming out. I just hid out in the woods and snuck back here."

Harvey stuck the money in his pocket. "Let's get busy, C. M. We've got a lot to do. I can't go all day without something to eat. Just look at me. I'm nothing but skin and bones."

Rocky grinned. "Yeah, I guess you're right. Okay, I'll look for the tent. Call me when the stew is ready."

Harvey heaped more wood on the fire, poured the stew in a pot and added water. Then he made an aluminum oven. He mixed the corn meal with water and poured the batter into the frying pan. The corn pie went into the oven for baking.

A glance toward the sun told him it was

almost noon. His stomach grumbled. He poured some water into a cup, dropped in a fizzie and sipped the flavored water.

Rocky returned. "I've looked everywhere and can't find the tent. I'll bet it's floated to the Mississippi River by now. But I found the tree that was hit by lightning. It is really shattered." He looked into the pot of stew. "This stuff ready yet?"

"Should be very soon. Want a fizzie?"

Rocky shook his head. He picked up a fish pole. "What are we going to use as bait? Worms?"

"Why not. The ground is full of them."

"Okay. I'll dig for bait. Call me when the stew is ready."

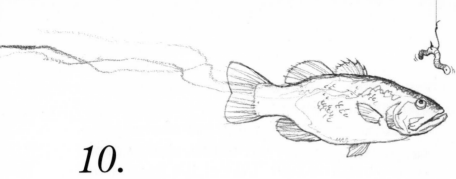

10.
A Big One

For more than an hour they fished from the boulders at the south end of the island. The hot sun beat against the water as their floats bobbed in the ripples of the stream. During all this time they didn't have a single bite.

"There are no fish here," Rocky moaned.

"Sure there are, C. M. We know they're here. It's just that they aren't hungry. My guess is that the rain washed too much food into the river, and they have more than they can eat."

"Aren't they lucky. But what about us? What do we do? Eat worms?"

"I've been thinking, C. M. We could spear fish. I've seen it done on TV. If the fish won't come to us, we go to them."

"Okay. But where?"

"Out there." Harvey's arm swept over the river under the cliffs.

"But we can't just walk out there. We'd scare the fish away. And it's too far to swim over."

"I know. But we might make a raft, something to lie on. When we see a fish, pow! Just drop right down on him."

"Now you're talking." Rocky bounded up. "We can use the branches from the tree that the lightning shattered. Let's go. We don't have all day, you know."

Harvey laughed. He never had seen Rocky so eager to get to work. He pulled his line from the water and climbed the hill to the camp.

Rocky grabbed the hatchet and a pile of rope. "Bring the knife and fishing line." He ran down the Wisconsin side of the hill.

Harvey changed into bathing trunks, picked up the knife and fishing line. He hurried to join Rocky.

Together they chopped and stripped the branches of the shattered tree. Then they pulled them to the beach on the Wisconsin

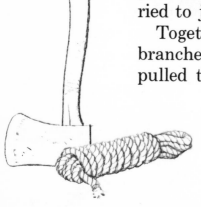

94

side of the island. They lashed the ends of the logs with rope to make a big square. With the long thin branches, they made a big X. Using fishing line, they lashed the branches to the logs.

Pushing the raft off the beach and into the water, Rocky crawled to the center. It slowly sank under his weight and scrapped the bottom.

"You try it, Harvey, I'm too heavy."

Harvey jumped onto the branches. His weight forced the raft underwater, but it floated and started. Sticking his face in the water, he opened his eyes.

Rocky grabbed the raft and pushed it back to the river bank. "I think it'll work. I'll hang on and swim in the back. When you see a fish, let me know. I'll get it."

"Okay, C. M. Make some spears. I'm going to get the plastic wrap so we can make some face masks. The water is pretty dirty."

Getting the film, Harvey tore off a piece and smoothed it against his forehead. He covered his ears and nose and eyes and pressed it against his cheeks. Breathing through his

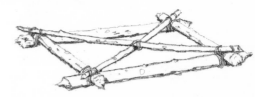

mouth, the film stuck to his skin. He had a mask.

He gave some of the film to Rocky who did the same. Each boy took two sharp sticks. Pushing the raft, they got it back into the stream.

Wading behind the raft, they aimed for the Wisconsin shore. The water got deeper and deeper. When it reached his chest, Harvey pulled himself onto the raft. He worked his way to the middle.

Rocky hung onto the raft with his hands. He kicked his feet. He acted as a rudder and as a motor.

Harvey stuck his face in the water. The sun sifted through the murky depths. Many small fish swam by. Then a large bass came into view. Harvey held up his arm. The fish saw the raft and darted out of view.

Harvey lifted his face. "You scared a big one away. Let's just coast."

"Okay."

"When I raise my arm, I've spotted a big one. I'll point to where he is. You go after him. Okay?"

Slowly the raft drifted downstream. Rocky guided it closer and closer to the Wisconsin cliffs.

Suddenly, Harvey saw a large catfish. His arm shot up. He pointed to the rear corner of the raft.

Rocky dropped his face into the water to find the fish. He sank.

The raft hung over the scene of the battle. Harvey watched as Rocky missed with the first stab. The fish turned to ride with the current. Rocky tried again. He caught the fish below the back fin.

The catfish spun in the water. The spear bent, twisted, and snapped. Part of the spear stayed in the fish. The other part was in Rocky's hand. He dropped the broken spear. He aimed with his second spear, stabbing the fish in the gills. Blood spurted into the water. The fish spun and twisted.

Rocky dropped the spear, grabbed the raft and panted. "I'm winded. Finish him off."

"Okay." Harvey scrambled off the raft and into the water.

The trail of dark stain led him to the catfish. Aiming his own spear, he stabbed through the center of the body. The weak fish twisted as Harvey pulled against the spear. He felt his lungs aching for air as he headed for the raft, still holding the spear.

Rocky dropped underwater to grab his own spear. Together, they pulled the fish from the water. They tossed the bleeding fish onto the raft and interlocked the spears into the logs.

"That's a nice one," Rocky panted. "We'll have dinner tonight."

"Nice one?" Harvey felt his stomach rumble. "He looks ugly. You mean you'll eat that thing?"

"Sure. Some of my friends say it is the best fish they've ever tasted. I'll show you. I might be a lousy cook with food, but I sure know how to cook fish. We'll have a real meal."

"Yeah. If we get back, that is. How are we going to get back?"

The raft had drifted past the cliffs. The river narrowed, and the current churned and rumbled, pushing the raft faster and faster.

"Just aim for the Minnesota shore. Don't worry about the current. We can walk back."

Soon the raft reached the shore and bumped into the bank.

Rocky pulled the raft part way up the bank and tossed the fish to the ground. Harvey untied all the rope and let the logs float away. Both boys rested a few minutes before heading back to camp.

11.
Fish Heads

On the long hike back up the river bank, Harvey spotted a dark green patch of cloth caught on a snag of brush. It was the tent. He pulled it free. The tent was torn and most of the buttons were missing. With Rocky's help, he shook it out and folded it up.

"Maybe we can mend it."

Rocky snorted. "You're out of your mind."

"Well, I'm glad we found it anyway."

When they arrived at the beach facing their island, Rocky plowed into the river. He took five steps before his shin struck a hidden rock. "Yikes," he yelled as he flipped into the water.

The catfish spun off his shoulder and started floating downstream.

Harvey dropped the tent and ropes and ran down the bank. Carefully, he stepped out into the stream feeling his way with his bare toes. He let the catfish float down to him, grabbed it, and waded over to the island.

Rocky was drying himself off on the beach. His shin had an ugly red scratch.

Harvey shook his head. "You better put some iodine on that cut. That water is pretty dirty. Take the fish to camp. I'll go back for the tent."

When they were both at camp, Rocky put the catfish on a piece of log. He pulled the spears from the jagged holes.

Harvey's mouth quivered as he stared at the ugly fish. The big, dark, gaping mouth seemed to hiss. The long tapering whiskers jiggled and waved in the air with each tug by Rocky. The wide-open dead eyes stared as they followed his every move.

"Hold the tail, Harvey. But be careful and use a towel. That tail is sharp, and the backbone can really cut." Rocky jabbed the knife behind the head. He sawed, poked, and jabbed. The blood oozed over the knife blade. He pried and chipped through the backbone. The head rolled to the ground.

Harvey turned to look away.

Rocky grabbed the long whiskers. "Ain't he a beaut? You know what I'm going to do? I'm going to save it. When we get back to camp, I'm going to stuff it into Steve's sleeping bag. Wow! Won't he get a shock?"

Harvey cringed. "That's a silly idea. Throw it away. It's ugly. I'm going to be sick."

Rocky laughed. He covered the fish head with plastic wrap and tucked it under his sleeping bag for safekeeping.

He picked up the knife. "Now the juicy part."

He stabbed the skin below the breastbone and sliced the fish open down the middle. Over a piece of plastic film, he spilled the innards of the fish.

Harvey held his stomach with his left hand. He just knew he was going to be sick. His eyes were trapped by the sliding guts, heart, liver, and blood of the messy insides.

Rocky laughed as he wrapped the shiny wet intestines in the plastic film. "What do you say we play catch? The one that drops it would really be sorry."

102

"No thanks." Harvey turned to sink to the ground. He gagged. His stomach churned.

"Get me some water, will you? I want to wash these fish steaks I'm going to cut."

Harvey crawled to the pail, took a deep breath, and poured in some of their drinking water from the canteen. Without looking at the fish again, he put the pail by Rocky.

He unrolled the torn tent and inspected it closely. Checking his supplies in the box, he tried to find a way to mend the tent. The things he needed weren't there. He smoothed

the tent out as best as he could and folded
it up for the last time.

He kept busy at the storage box, throwing
the last of the spoiled food into the garbage
pit. Anything to keep away from the messy
fish-chopping job that Rocky was engaged in.
Never having caught a catfish before, Harvey
hadn't expected such a gory sight.

Rocky threw the last of the fish into the
garbage pit. A pile of fish steaks rested on a
plate.

Harvey brought his chair over to watch as
Rocky dabbed salt and pepper on the white
meat. Then he pressed the steaks into the
cornmeal to cover both sides.

There were still hot coals left from the fire
Harvey had made to cook the stew.

Rocky preheated the frying pan. Then he
spread the meat in the pan. Every few minutes he turned the steaks to fry them golden
brown on both sides.

"How come they don't stick?"

"Catfish has its own fat." Rocky scooped
a steak onto a plate and handed it to Harvey.
"Chow is now ready."

104

Harvey cut a small piece of the steaming fish and tasted it. He nodded. "Why, this is good, C. M."

"I told you. Tastes like bass."

Harvey poured some syrup on the corn-bread left from breakfast and ate more of the fish. "This is better than the stew. And it's not even burnt. Looks like you've finally learned how to cook."

"I've been cooking catfish long before this summer."

Rocky took the last strip from the pan and added a fresh batch. "I'm going to eat till I burst. I figure this is our last meal."

"I'll have some more, too. Maybe we should have started living off the land sooner. I think this is the best meal we've had."

Harvey heard a noise. He rose and looked toward the beach. "Hey, C. M. It's Mr. Adams." He whispered hoarsely, "Quick. Clean up any mess."

The canoe ground to a stop on the beach. Mr. Adams stepped out carrying a clipboard and pulled the canoe farther up the bank. He walked up to the camp.

"Howdy, Team Ten. Everything going all right?"

"Sure is," Harvey smiled.

Rocky nodded. "We're having catfish steaks. We've got more than enough. Do you want some?"

"Don't mind if I do. My, you've made some chairs. Good. All the comforts of home." He sat, took the plate and tasted the fish. "This is good. Very good."

"We had to go spearfishing to get him." Rocky stood up. He tried cleaning his hands by rubbing them against his trunks.

"Our tent got ripped up by the storm last night. We found it, but it's too torn up for me to mend. That's why it isn't up."

"I see." Mr. Adams rose, and slowly walked around the camp. He kept putting check marks on the paper on the clipboard.

Harvey watched and noticed each item that Mr. Adams inspected. His heart was pounding fast, but he stood still, mentally crossing his fingers, just hoping. He noticed Rocky putting the dirty dishes into the wash water bubbling on the fire.

Mr. Adams paused for several moments before the storage box. He closed the lid, checked his paper, and came back to the boys. "Think you can last till morning?"

"You bet," Harvey stated.

"Don't see why not," Rocky said.

"Okay. But if it gets too tough, just call in. Anybody sick or hurt?"

"No," Harvey said. Then he saw Mr. Adams staring at the cut on Rocky's leg.

Rocky raised his leg to rub the cut. "It's all right, Mr. Adams. Bruised it against a rock when we were after the catfish."

Mr. Adams bent down to take a look at the cut. "Looks okay, I guess. Okay, Team Ten. I'll see you in the morning."

They watched as Mr. Adams returned to the canoe, pushed off and paddled back upstream.

"How do you think we made out?" Harvey asked.

"I don't know. We'll know tomorrow."

"Yeah. Guess we will."

12.

Fire Ants

Harvey lit the tin-can candle and set it down by his bedroll. He crawled into his blankets and lay down. He watched the trees overhead as they rustled in the light breeze. It felt good sleeping in the open, and he was sorry he hadn't tried it before.

Rocky, still in his bathing suit, was playing at the fire.

"Better get to bed, C. M. We have to clean up the camp in the morning."

"Later." He threw more pine cones on the fire.

Harvey blew out the candle and curled up to sleep. It seemed only a moment later that he jerked awake. Rocky had stumbled over his foot.

"Sorry." Rocky lit the candle.

He jerked the zipper of his mummy bag, slid in, and with several yanks pulled the zipper up. He slid his feet to the bottom, kicking against the catfish head he had hidden under the bag. He leaned over to blow the candle out, then he stopped.

Slowly at first, and then faster and faster, he thrashed his legs about. Then, madly, he tore at the zipper.

"Help! There's something in my sleeping bag! It's eating me up!"

Fully awake, Harvey sat up.

"Get me out of here! There's animals in my bag. They're eating me up!"

Rocky bucked and jerked, rolled and thrashed about.

Harvey jumped out of his blankets to help with the stuck zipper.

"It's wildcats in here. They're chewing me up," Rocky screamed. His foot poked out of the burnt hole, then disappeared back inside the bag.

Harvey's fingers tore at the zipper. He yanked and pulled to free it.

Rocky ripped the bag from his body and

saw all the red fire ants covering his feet and legs. He sped down the path and with one dive ended deep in the water of the river.

Harvey turned on his flashlight.

The plastic-wrapped fish head was hidden by layer after layer of red ants chewing into the flesh of the fish. A heavy mass of ants poured from the sleeping bag.

Carefully holding the bag away from him, he pulled the zipper down the full length. He turned the bag inside out. The last of the marshmallows were caught in the foot of the bag. To them clung an ant hill of fire ants.

He tossed the sleeping bag as best as he could. The marshmallows fell to the ground. Most of the ants fell out. He tossed the bag to Rocky when he came back.

"I told you not to eat in your sleeping bag. That's what did it. It was just like sleeping on an ant hill."

Rocky stared at the bag. His hand rubbed the red welts that covered his legs and feet. "Yikes."

"Put it on the clothes line and beat it with a stick. That should get all the ants out."

He took the shovel to scoop up the ant-covered fish head and marshmallows and dropped them in the garbage pit. Using the shovel as a broom, he swept the camp area free of ants.

Rocky closely checked his sleeping bag. He brought it back to camp, put on his pajamas and crawled into the bag. "What a day. I'll be glad to get back to camp tomorrow."

"Me, too." Harvey blew out the candle and went back to sleep.

*　　*　　*

The early morning sun peeped through the trees to wake Harvey. He sat up, rubbed his eyes and looked around the camp.

Crawling from his blankets, he started to nudge Rocky, but didn't. Rocky didn't really care how the island looked. Why argue with him?

He checked the fire pit. It was out. But he didn't really need a fire. There wasn't anything to eat.

He changed into his clothes, and put all of

112

his gear into his knapsack. Then he stored the cleaned dishes in the box. He filled the garbage pit, cleaned up the fireplace, and took down the clothes line.

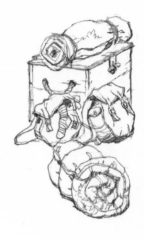

At last, everything but the latrine was done. The island looked almost the way they had found it. Their only loss was the torn tent.

Looking up the river, he saw Mr. Adams paddling toward the island. He prodded Rocky. "Wake up, C. M. Mr. Adams is coming."

*   *   *

That night they sat around the campfire at the base camp. Harvey's heart pounded. He didn't really know, but he figured that he and Rocky had a chance for the medal. Some of the teams had been caught at the store. Other teams had quit during the storm. He didn't know how many teams had finished the three days, but he and Rocky were one of the teams.

Mr. Adams raised his hand for quiet.

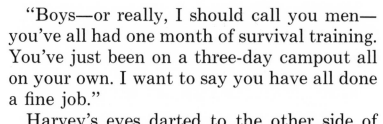

"Boys—or really, I should call you men—you've all had one month of survival training. You've just been on a three-day campout all on your own. I want to say you have all done a fine job."

Harvey's eyes darted to the other side of the fire. Rocky sat with his tentmates.

"We did find two teams at the store. That wasn't right. We had one team quit early, but that's normal. This is a tough test. If they come back next year, I'm sure they will be our star leaders."

Harvey clicked it off in his mind. Two teams caught at the store and one team quit. That accounts for three so far.

"Then in that rainstorm, we had to rescue two teams. Nothing to feel bad about. According to our records, that was the worst storm we've ever had."

Mr. Adams looked around the circle of boys. Then he continued.

"Two more teams were unable to get any food for their last day. The storm had washed out their supplies. They came into camp last night."

Harvey's eyes grew wide. Seven teams so far. Team Ten was one of the three teams that had lasted the three days.

"Will Team Ten come up front please?" Mr. Adams smiled.

In a daze Harvey stood up. He stepped out. Rocky joined him. The two boys looked at each other and smiled. Rocky's legs still had welts from the ant bites.

"You two boys have won the medal as best campers. Your camp was in the best shape. You fed yourselves when you ran out of food. You had a terrible test in that rainstorm as well."

Mr. Adams placed a loop of blue ribbon over Harvey's head. The circular bronze medal dropped against his chest.

Harvey touched the medal.

He had won something at last. But he knew he had won much more than a medal. He had won a contest, a contest with himself, and a contest with other boys. He knew his parents and his uncle Leon would be proud of him.

He looked at Rocky, who also held his medal. "I'll tell you something, C. M. You won that medal by working—not by being the biggest."

"Yeah."

The two boys smiled at each other and shook hands.

About the Author

George S. Cook was born in Chicago, Illinois. He has lived in Washington, D.C., New York, and Minnesota before moving to California.

He is a graduate, with a degree in chemistry, of George Washington University and is presently employed as sales manager for the Chemical Coatings Corporation.

His many years of experience in scouting and as Scoutmaster led to the writing of this book.

When he and his family are not camping, Mr. Cook enjoys performing in plays presented by drama groups at the Little Theater.

Mr. and Mrs. Cook and their five children live in Santa Ana, California.

About the Illustrator

Herman Beeson Vestal was born in New York City. He grew up in North Carolina, New Mexico, Virginia, Canada, and Florida, and presently resides in New Jersey.

He has been a free-lance illustrator for a number of years, illustrating numerous children's books and textbooks.

Mr. Vestal and his son, along with the family Golden Retriever have enjoyed camping in the Adirondacks, and hope, in the not too distant future, to portage in Canada.